Penguin  Readers

T0332759

JAZ SANTOS VS THE WORLD

PRISCILLA MANTE

LEVEL

RETOLD BY MAEVE CLARKE
ILLUSTRATED BY ANGLIKA DEWI ANGGREINI
SERIES EDITOR: SORREL PITTS

PENGUIN BOOKS

UK | USA | Canada | Ireland | Australia
India | New Zealand | South Africa

Penguin Books is part of the Penguin Random House group of companies
whose addresses can be found at global.penguinrandomhouse.com.
www.penguin.co.uk www.puffin.co.uk www.ladybird.co.uk

Penguin
Random House
UK

Jaz Santos vs the World first published by Puffin Books, 2021
This Penguin Readers edition published by Penguin Books Ltd, 2024
001

Original text written by Priscilla Mante
Text for Penguin Readers edition adapted by Maeve Clarke
Original copyright © Priscilla Mante, 2021
Text for Penguin Readers edition copyright © Penguin Books Ltd, 2024
Illustrated by Anglika Dewi Anggreini
Illustrations copyright © Penguin Books Ltd, 2024
Cover image copyright © Camilla Sucre, 2021
Design project management by Dynamo Limited

The moral right of the original author has been asserted

Printed and bound in Great Britain by Clays Ltd, Elcograf S.p.A.

The authorized representative in the EEA is Penguin Random House Ireland,
Morrison Chambers, 32 Nassau Street, Dublin D02 YH68

A CIP catalogue record for this book is available from the British Library

ISBN: 978–0–241–63678–7

All correspondence to:
Penguin Books
Penguin Random House Children's
One Embassy Gardens, 8 Viaduct Gardens,
London SW11 7BW

Contents

People in the story

The Santos-Campbell family

Mum/Mãe   Dad   Jordan

Jaz

Rosie

The Bramrock Stars

Charligh   Naomie   Steph   Talia

Allie   Layla   Rhiannon

New words

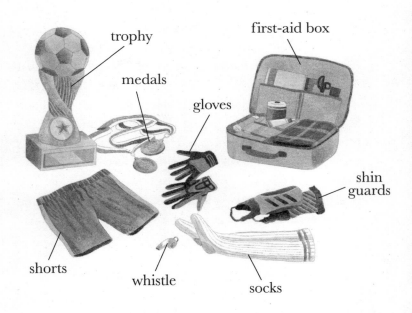

trophy

first-aid box

medals

gloves

shin guards

shorts

whistle

socks

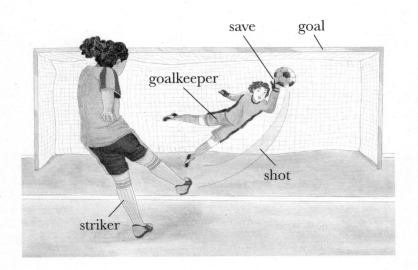

save

goal

goalkeeper

striker

shot

Note about the story

Priscilla Mante is from Scotland. Now she lives in London. *Jaz Santos vs the World* is her first book.

Ten-year-old Jaz and her friends all have big **dreams***. Jaz loves playing football, but many people think that football is only for boys. Jaz's parents **argue** a lot. Jaz thinks that this is because she is always in trouble at school. She hopes that, if she wins a football **tournament**, her parents will love her more, and that they will stop arguing. So she makes a football **team** with her friends. They want to show that girls can do the same things as boys. This story is about hope and being **brave**. It is also about following your dreams and reaching for the **stars**.

Before-reading questions

1 *Jaz Santos vs the World*. What does this title mean, do you think?

2 Choose three people from the "People in the story" on page 4. Who are they and what are they like, do you think? Think about:

- How old are they?
- What are their hobbies and interests?
- What makes them happy?
- What are their dreams?

3 Which sports do you like to play?

*Definitions of words in **bold** can be found in the glossary on pages 78–80.

I'm Jaz!

Hi! My name's Jasmina Santos-Campbell, but everyone calls me Jaz. When I'm in trouble, they call me Jasmina. Have you heard of me and the Bramrock **Stars**? We're *almost* famous. This is our story.

―――――

Charligh is my best friend and we go to Ms Morgan's after-school dance lesson twice a week.

"This is our last chance to show Ms Morgan that we can dance well, Charligh," I said. "Today, she'll choose us to dance in *Spinning Alices* – our school end-of-year **show**."

"Everyone knows that *I'm* the best dancer," said Rosie Calderwood. "I'll be the star dancer." Rosie is the opposite to a friend – she's an enemy.

"Ms Morgan will choose Rosie," said Erica. Erica always agrees with Rosie.

"Girls," Ms Morgan said. "Show me your dances."

I wanted to be the star dancer because, first, I really wanted Mãe – that's Mum in Portuguese – to be **proud** of me. And, second, Mãe was making the clothes for the show. This was my second year at dance class and I still danced like an **elephant**. This year had to be different because Mãe and Dad were **arguing** a lot at home.

I was trying to pirouette – that means to quickly turn round in a circle. Suddenly, I fell past one of the other girls and my arm hit the wall. I laughed, but Ms Morgan didn't think that it was funny.

"Sit over there, Jaz," she said. "You can come back in five minutes."

Rosie smiled, and I felt very stupid.

It was boring to watch the others dance, so I thought about playing football for England in the Women's World Cup **final**.

*And Jaz Santos **scores** a goal in the **final** minute!*

People are shouting . . . Jaz! Jaz!

"Jaz! *Jasmina!!*" Ms Morgan said. "Come and dance now, please."

At the end of the class, Ms Morgan asked me to wait. I knew that she wanted me to be the star dancer. "Rosie will be very unhappy," I thought.

"Jaz! What am I going to say to you?" asked Ms Morgan.

I didn't know. That was the problem. But Ms Morgan wasn't smiling. Maybe I wasn't the star dancer.

"You can be a good dancer, but you must work harder," said Ms Morgan. "You're 'on report' for the next week. This means that I'll watch you very closely and I'm going to speak to all your other teachers."

Oh no! I had to be good for one week.

"I can do this," I thought, "if I try hard."

———

Mãe forgot to come to dance class for me. Again. This isn't a big problem because my mum's the Coolest Mum. She speaks Portuguese and English. She doesn't talk to me about homework, and she makes and wears beautiful headwraps. People like the clothes that she makes. Now she's with her **customers** all the time, and not with me and my brother, Jordan.

When I got home, I ran into Mãe's work room. She was sitting at the huge desk that Dad made for her, and she was drawing new ideas for her clothes. She saw me, and she put her hand to her head.

"Jaz! I'm sorry. I forgot to meet you at school. How was dance?"

"OK," I said. I didn't want to tell her that I might not be the star dancer in the show.

"Are you hungry? Do you want me to cook something?"

"No," I said, quickly. Mãe's a terrible cook! My dad loves cooking different things.

"OK, dear," she said and turned back to her drawings.

––––––

That evening, we all had dinner together. My parents weren't arguing tonight, and I didn't want this to change.

"Ms Morgan thinks that I can be one of the best dancers," I said. This was almost true, I thought.

"You didn't tell me this before," Mãe said. A smile danced across her face. "Now I'll have to make a special dress for the best dancer."

After dinner, I **practised** football in the garden. Football made everything better. In school, at dance, at home . . . I was always making mistakes. But on the football field – I understood the game. I could **dribble** and strike very well. I practised **keepy-uppies**. I could do thirty-three without stopping. "Girls can't play football," says Zach Bacon, from my school. But he can only do thirty-one keepy-uppies.

———

I was in bed and trying to sleep, but my parents were arguing. I went downstairs very quietly to listen to them.

Suddenly, Dad opened the living room door. "Are you all right, Jaz?" he asked. "It's very late."

"I wanted a drink," I said, quickly. I didn't want to say that the **argument** was stopping me from sleeping.

When I went back to bed, the house was very quiet. Later, I heard only one of my parents come upstairs to bed.

———

The next day at school, I played football with the boys at lunchtime. Some of the boys didn't like girls that played better than them, so they wouldn't **pass** the ball to me.

That afternoon in class, we had to make a cake.

"The best **cinnamon** and apple cake will win a **prize**," said Mrs Tavella, the cooking teacher.

"Rosie makes the best cakes," Erica said. But we knew that Erica was **lying** because her ears turned pink.

Charligh and I worked hard to make a good cake mix. Then, I went to look at Rosie and Erica's cake mix – it looked good. So I added something different to our cake mix to make it better. We cooked it and it looked lovely.

"Your cake looks really horrible," Rosie said.

"Try it," I said.

Rosie ate a big slice. Suddenly, her face was grey and green. Then, she was sick! It smelled horrible. Some of her sick fell on Erica's arm and now Erica was looking green, too.

Everybody stepped back, holding their noses. Rosie pointed straight at me.

"Jaz did it!" she said. "She made me sick."

CHAPTER TWO
Fire!

"It was a mistake," I said. "I wanted to put cinnamon in the cake, but I put in hot chilli."

Mrs Forrest, one of our most important teachers, came into the room. "You've made Rosie and Erica sick!" she shouted.

"The smell of Rosie's sick made Erica sick," said Charligh. "So Rosie is half the problem."

Mrs Forrest smiled. I didn't like her smile. A happy Mrs Forrest was always unhappy news for me.

"You're already on report this week, Jasmina!" she said. "I'm going to tell Ms Morgan that you can't go to dance lessons until after the holidays."

"Then I'm leaving the dance class, too," said Charligh.

This was worse than terrible. "But we have to be in the dance show this year," I said.

"Don't say another word," Mrs Forrest replied. "School has finished for today. Go home. NOW!"

I tried not to cry. Why did I always make things worse?

———

On Fridays, I often went to dinner at Charligh's house. Tonight, we were ready to eat, but suddenly my dad rang at the front door.

"Don't worry," he said to me. "But there has been a fire at the house. The firefighters are there and everyone's safe. Jordan was at band **practice**."

"What happened? Was Mãe in the house?"

"Yes," Dad said.

Charligh's mum looked at my dad. And then he looked at Charligh's mum. Adults think that children can't see that special look.

"You can stay here tonight," Charligh's mum said to me.

"Thank you," I replied, "but I'd like to go home now."

———

Dad and I arrived home, and everything looked almost normal. The firefighters were in the garden and Mãe was smoking a cigarette. She saw me, put the cigarette under her foot and **hugged** me.

"Are you OK, Mãe?"

"I was smoking a cigarette in the living room," she explained. "I fell asleep for five minutes."

"Did we lose anything in the fire?"

"Only some of your dad's papers. The firefighters were very quick."

"Five minutes is all you need for the house to catch fire, Iris," Dad said in a cold voice.

Mãe looked at Dad. "I'm sorry that I'm not wonderful like you, Drew," she said, angrily. She didn't sound sorry.

"You were very lucky this time," one of the firefighters said to Dad. "You have children, and if this happens again . . ." Dad's face turned red.

"Did you hear that?" Dad asked Mãe when we walked back to the house.

"Of course," Mãe replied. "I've got ears, you know that."

I didn't like seeing my parents like this, and I went inside and ran upstairs to my bedroom. There was a message from Charligh on my phone.

> **Charligh:** Are u OK? x

> **Jaz:** Yes. We're all OK. It was cool to have firefighters in my garden. x

> **Charligh:** You're so lucky. x

I started to write "*No, I'm not*" – I didn't want to tell **lies** any more . . . but I heard a noise at my door and I quickly wrote.

> **Jaz:** Jordan's here. Speak to you later x

> **Charligh:** Tell him that I said hi :)
> Speak to you tomorrow x

Jordan came in, opened my window and then sat on the floor.

"Let's play Favourites," he said. This was strange because, two years ago, Jordan thought that he was too old to play this game with me.

We played for a few minutes, but soon we heard our parents arguing again.

"You've changed," I heard, and, "Everything is always about you." Then, we heard Mãe crying and speaking very quickly on the phone in Portuguese.

Jordan went back to his room, and I hugged Kinsley, my toy elephant. After a while, Mãe came to my door. Her eyes were red.

"Please come down to the living room," she said.

———————

Now I was sitting on the sofa with Jordan.

"Your mum's going to stay with Aunty Bella," Dad said.

"So?" I replied. "Mãe stays with Tia Bella all the time." *Tia* is Portuguese for aunt. I hoped that this was normal, but I knew that it wasn't. "Are you coming back tomorrow, or the day after that, or the day after the day after tomorrow?" I kept talking because then I couldn't hear anything that I didn't want to hear.

"I . . . we . . . aren't sure," Mãe said, softly. She stood up, and her chair made a loud noise on the wood floor. "Look after your sister, Jordan," she said.

Jordan looked very surprised, then he stood up.

"Don't worry. I'll look after Jaz. Have a nice time with Tia," he said.

Have a nice time with Aunty? Didn't my brother understand? Mãe wasn't going on a happy holiday. She was leaving us.

Why didn't Dad do something? Maybe I could say that I was sick – just until tomorrow.

"If you need anything –" Mãe kissed the top of my head – "then call me and I'll be there."

Mãe didn't understand. I needed *her*. I needed her *here* at home. "She's leaving because I'm not in *Spinning Alices*," I thought. "And I wasn't good enough to stay in dance class. I'm never good enough."

––––––––

That Saturday morning, our house felt very quiet. Dad was cleaning, and I went to the park. I wanted to play football with the Year 6 boys.

Theo saw me arrive. "Sorry," he said. "We're practising for a **tournament**. Only the school **team** can play."

This made me very angry. I wasn't on the team because I was a girl!

"Go away, Jaz!" said Zach. I tried to kick the ball by his feet, but I fell on the wet grass and the boys all laughed at me.

I went home and had a shower. Dad made two cups of hot chocolate and we had a talk. I told him everything about the dance class, the cake and Rosie being sick. That evening, we played **video** games and we made Dad's Special Pizza together.

"Why can't life be as easy as making pizza?" he said, quietly.

I didn't have the answer.

CHAPTER THREE

The sleepover

I was waiting for Charligh in Bramrock library. A young woman called Rhiannon was trying to put some **flyers** in the correct places on the wall. There were a lot of people waiting for her at the library desk.

"I can do this," I said, pointing at the flyers, "and you can talk to the customers."

Rhiannon smiled. "Thanks."

"My name's Jaz," I said.

I put all the flyers into the correct places. Then, I saw the last one. It said,

BRIGHTON GIRLS' UNDER 11S SEVEN-A-SIDE
FOOTBALL TOURNAMENT
CLOSING DATE 7 OCTOBER

A football tournament for primary schools! The only thing that I was good at was football. I looked at the website on my phone, and there were lots of pictures of women and girls playing football. There was also a lot of information about the tournament

Charligh arrived and I showed her the flyer.

"Look! It's a girls' football tournament. Let's start our own team?"

"Why?" asked Charligh.

I showed her the prize on my phone, and she smiled.

> **FIRST PRIZE**
>
> Two hundred and fifty pounds for sports clothes
>
> Your name in the *Brighton Chronicle* **newspaper**
>
> Winners' medals
>
> Brighton Girls' Under 11s Seven-a-Side Football Tournament trophy.

"If we win, we'll be famous, *and* the Year 6 boys will be angry," said Charligh. "Let's do it!"

I went home. "How can I get more people on the team?" I thought. "Half of the girls in my class don't like football." Suddenly, I had an idea.

"Can I have a sleepover, Dad?"

Dad tried not to laugh. "How many people do you want to sleep in our house for one night?"

"Nine," I replied.

"*How* many?" Dad looked a bit frightened. "You can invite six."

I only needed six. I wrote six cards. Jordan came with me because it was nearly dark outside.

First, we left cards at Naomie's house and at Steph's house because they lived on the same street. The next house was Charligh's.

"Hello," she said.

I gave her the card. She kept looking and smiling at Jordan. "I'll be there," she said. That night, Naomie and Steph sent me phone messages saying "yes". Now there were four people on my team.

The next day at school, I found Talia Janowicz during the morning break. She was sitting in the school garden looking at her chess set. I didn't know Talia very well, but she sometimes played football.

I gave Talia the card and she read it carefully. "Thanks," she said. "I'll be there." Then, she looked at her chess set again.

The next person I asked was Allie Norton because she was good at some ball games. Allie got angry very easily. She was in more trouble at school than me! She was sitting next to her best (and only) friend, Layla Hussani. Layla loved anything that was pink.

"I'm having a sleepover this Saturday," I said to Allie. "It's a football party."

"Are you serious?" Allie asked.

"We'll be there," Layla said, quickly.

The card wasn't really for Layla. I didn't think that she liked football – but I was happy to have her. Now I had my team.

————

On Saturday, Dad and I got everything ready. I was very excited and a little frightened. I had to make this the best sleepover EVER. I wanted them to see that football was great.

Everybody arrived, and we watched a film called *Flo's Football Fame*. It was about Florrie Redford. She played for the first women's football team, a long time ago. People then had stupid ideas.

"Women can't play football," they said. "Only men can play." At the end of the film, all my friends **cheered**.

"Those people were wrong," said Charligh. "Of course women can play football!"

"People still say things like that now," Layla replied. "It's called being sexist."

"My uncle Gavin's sexist," Allie told us. "He says that I can't be a builder because I'm a girl."

"We can be anything that we want to be," said Steph.

"Yes, we can," I agreed. "There are lots of **professional** women football players all around the world. They aren't as famous as the men players, but they're just as good."

Just before midnight, Dad made us go to bed and kissed me goodnight. I smiled. My dad was here, and he wasn't going anywhere. I had best friends. All I needed was for Mãe to come home.

———

The next day, we all went to the park to play football.

My friends were terrible. Layla quickly forgot that she was in my team, and she passed the ball to Allie. Then, Naomie scored a goal for the wrong team. After that, they all kicked the ball anywhere. At the end of the game, they all cheered. I couldn't **believe** it.

We got home, and I showed them the tournament website on my phone. Everybody wanted to be on the team. Now we needed a name. "What about the Stars?" I said.

"The Bramrock Stars!" they all shouted. And then they asked me to be the **captain**. Me!

I felt frightened, proud and excited. The tournament was in eight weeks, so we didn't have much time to practise. But I thought about Mãe living with Tia, and it made me want to win even more. I wanted Mãe at home with us.

"Because mums always come back," I thought.

At lunchtime the next day, I went to see Miss Williams, our class teacher. I told her everything about the Bramrock Stars and the tournament.

"Miss Williams, will you help us?"

"Yes," said Miss Williams. "I don't know much about football, but I'd love to help."

———

After school, Miss Williams gave us some good news.

"You're in the tournament now," she said. Everybody cheered. "But I have bad news, too. The school has spent all its money on the boys' team. But we can use the boys' old football shirts."

At home, I tried to video call Mãe three times, but she didn't answer, so I sent her an email.

Hi Mãe

I'm sorry that I'm not going to be in the dance show, but I'm in a girls' football tournament! And that's better! Our team is the Bramrock Stars FC. You can come and **cheer** for us in the final.

I **miss** you a lot.

Jaz XXX

CHAPTER FOUR
A new coach

I looked out of the car window. Dad was driving me to visit Mãe and Tia for the night.

"You normally love visiting Aunty Bella," he said, looking at my face.

"Yes, but Mãe is in Tia's world more than she is in ours, now," I thought.

"Oh, Jaz!" Mãe hugged me, but I couldn't hug her back. She felt different. Nobody spoke for a minute. Then, Mãe said, "I'll take Jaz to school tomorrow."

"If you're sure . . ." Dad began.

"I'm sure!"

I felt uncomfortable. Tia looked at Dad and then held the front door open wide.

"Bye, Jaz," Dad said. "Have fun!"

"**Finally**," Tia said. "I thought that he didn't want to leave."

I felt terrible. Half of me wanted to run after Dad and the other half wanted to stay with Mãe.

"Can you smell the candles?" Mãe asked. She sat next to me on the sofa. "I've stopped smoking, and now I can smell everything."

I felt strange inside. Dad, Jordan and I asked her to stop smoking many times. Why did she stop now? I still remembered the fire at our house *that* day.

"How are the Bramrock Stars?" Mãe asked. "I'm very excited to see your team play."

"I'm going to be the captain."

"That's wonderful," Tia said. "Let's do something special with your hair."

Tia did my hair in cornrows. It looked beautiful. At dinner, Mum and Tia talked about Marcus – Mãe's old boyfriend – and I didn't like this. Did they think that Mãe's life with me and Dad and Jordan was very boring? Then, they saw my face and they stopped talking.

"I'm going to bed," I said.

"But it's only nine o'clock," replied Tia.

"I have school tomorrow," I replied.

Then, Tia asked a very important question. "Has your football team got a **coach**?"

It didn't. But I knew the right person to ask.

———

The next morning at school, I spoke to Mr Roundtree. He cleaned the school.

"Will you **coach** our football team?" I asked.

"No!" he said. "I'm already coaching the school team and you aren't on it. Girls and boys can't play together after Year 5."

"We've made our own team," I said. "We're going to play in the all-girls tournament."

"*You* are quite a good player . . . for a *girl*," said Mr Roundtree. "Good luck! You'll need it."

———

"I'll be the coach," I said to my friends.

I borrowed a *How to Play Football* book from the library. I needed to find some ideas for our next practice game.

———

I wanted us to play a 2-2-2 formation. The goalkeeper is in the goal, then the left and right backs – the defenders – are in the next line. The left and right midfielders are in front of them, and finally the left and right forwards. It was the simplest way to do things. But nobody liked their **position**.

We were terrible. Little by little, everybody got angrier and angrier. Then, Naomie kicked a ball into Charligh's face. It was a mistake, and Charligh was OK, but Allie laughed – a lot. Charligh was very, very angry. At the end of **training**, seven players walked off in seven different directions.

I got home, and I ran upstairs and hugged Kinsley.

"What are we going to do, Kinsley?" I asked. But, of course, Kinsley didn't have an answer.

———

I took the *How to Play Football* book back to the library.

"Did it help you?" asked Rhiannon.

"No."

"I'll be your coach," she said, suddenly.

I was very surprised. "Do you know anything about football?" I asked.

"Football's important in my family," she said.

"It's seven-a-side," I said, carefully. "It's different from a full team that has . . ."

"Eleven!" Rhiannon said. "Everyone knows *that*. Do you want my help or not?"

"We're training tomorrow in the park at 5 p.m."

"You're lucky," Rhiannon said. "I finish work at three. See you tomorrow."

———

Without her **make-up**, Rhiannon looked much younger.

"You're on Instagram!" Allie said.

"What do you mean?" I asked.

"Rhiannon's a big star on Instagram!" Allie said. "She's got about 20,000 followers. My big sister showed me. You study make-up art and you talk about make-up and food."

"Yes, I love food," Rhiannon said with a smile, "and we'll talk about it today."

Rhiannon explained that it was important to eat different foods to keep our bodies strong. Then, she talked about our positions in the team.

"Why is your position important and what would you like to practise most?" she asked.

Some said dribbling, and others said defending or **shooting**. Then, Rhiannon wrote a list of everything that we needed to bring with us next time.

Shin guards
Bottle of water
Football boots
Football clothes
Our **whole** selves

"These things will keep you safe, and help you play your best football," Rhiannon said.

"What does the last one mean?" Talia asked.

"It means that you all have different **strengths** and **skills** – but you must always be you," Rhiannon explained. "Jaz, you can dribble. Show us."

Because of Ms Morgan's dance lessons, I could now dribble very quickly.

Everybody left the training practice looking happier than the last time. My team didn't know it, but this was the start of trying to get my mum home.

CHAPTER FIVE
Football heroes

A lot of my teachers thought that I was lazy. But during the next few weeks, we all **trained** at the park every day after school. On Saturdays, we trained early in the morning, too.

———————

One Sunday afternoon, we played a friendly game with the women's team from Brighton University. There were about thirteen students on the field, all with different football skills.

"I want you to learn from them and they can learn from you," said Rhiannon.

"Do you think that they want to learn from us?" Allie asked. "Adults never listen to young people where I'm from."

"They really want to learn from you," Rhiannon replied.

Now we all had football boots, and Allie had shin guards and goalkeeper gloves. The best thing was that Mãe and Dad were both here to watch us. It was good to see them standing together without arguing. Team Blue was playing Team Yellow.

After that, Team Green was playing Team Red. Team Yellow was Allie, Steph and three university students. Team Blue was me and four university students. The other players in my team were really good.

I was one of the shortest players in Bramrock Stars and I felt even shorter here. It was five minutes before anybody on Team Blue passed the ball to me. Finally, I could go! *Right foot, left foot, right foot* . . . Then, I saw Mãe and Dad talking. Were they arguing? I lost **focus** and a Team Yellow player "stole" the ball from me.

A few seconds later, I had the ball again. This time, I wasn't going to lose it. Mãe and Dad were still not watching the game and I could see that Mãe was angry with Dad. I tried to score a goal, but Allie saved it. It was a good save from Allie and a bad **shot** from me.

After the game, I ran to Dad. Mãe wasn't with him.

"Where's Mãe?"

"Mum is sorry but she couldn't stay," Dad said and hugged me. "That was a great game, Jaz. You're a super striker!"

"I wasn't a super striker. I didn't score any goals,"

I thought. "Did Mãe leave early because I didn't score? Next time, I mustn't make any mistakes."

———

At our next training day, we practised dribbling and passing the ball. Then, we talked about our football heroes.

"Mine's David Seaman," Allie said. "He was the goalkeeper for England in the 1990s. He played for England seventy-five times. He had safe hands. That's his special skill."

"Every goalkeeper wants safe hands," Rhiannon said. "Becky Spencer is a great female goalkeeper. Watch videos of some of her saves."

"My hero's Raheem Sterling," said Steph. "He does a lot of good things to help people and defends the things that he **believes in**."

Rhiannon nodded. "The things a player does *off* the football field are as important as the things they do *on* the field. Because of that, some players become **role models** for young people."

"My favourite player's Megan Rapinoe," said Layla. "She's American. I like her because she's unpredictable – what will she do next? We don't know. And sometimes –" Layla smiled – "she has pink hair."

"If I can't be an actor," Charligh said, "then I want to be like Alex Scott. She was a defender for England. Now she talks about football on TV."

Finally, it was my **turn**. Before I could say a word, everybody shouted, "*Rachel Yankey!*"

"Hey," I said. "Maybe I want to choose another player."

"Who?" Naomie asked.

37

"OK." I laughed. "It *is* Rachel. She's fast and **skilful**. She's the best left forward ever and she played for England 129 times! If I don't choose Rachel, then maybe . . . Ji So-yun."

"Well done, girls." Rhiannon looked at her watch. "It's time for me to go to work, and I don't want to be late." She got on her bike and rode away.

Suddenly, Zach and his friends arrived. "Oi! Santos-Campbell," he shouted. "Move! We want to play here now!"

"We'll train for five more minutes, and then we'll go," Steph said.

Zach didn't look at Steph. He only looked at me. "I said NOW!"

My face began to get hot. Before I could speak, Layla stepped forward.

"We're not going anywhere," she said.

"Can you hear a little noise?" said Sebastian.

Allie and I moved and stood next to Layla. Zach took some rubbish and threw it all over us.

"You . . . !" Allie moved nearer Zach. She wanted to hit him, but Layla stopped her.

"Don't do anything, Allie," Layla said, trying not to cry. "They're trying to make problems for us."

Then, we all stood in front of Allie and Layla. After a long time, the boys moved to the other side of the park.

"Zach won't do that again," Naomie said, as we all went quickly to the café.

I always thought that Layla was quiet. Today, I discovered that she was a **brave** girl *and* that we really were a team – on the football field and off it.

CHAPTER SIX

Money

"We only have twenty-six pounds eighty-seven!" Steph said. "And we have to get a minibus to take us to the tournament." We were talking about the money that we needed for the Bramrock Stars. The most expensive thing was the minibus – a small bus.

"The cheapest minibus costs forty pounds an hour, and we need it for three hours!" said Steph.

"What are we going to do?" Talia asked.

"If we don't have a minibus, we can't go to the tournament," I said.

"This isn't **fair**. We have to pay for a minibus, *and* we've got the oldest and ugliest football shirts to wear," Allie said.

"The school has spent all the sports money on the boys' team. Now they need the school minibus to go to their own tournament," Naomie said. "They don't think that girls are important. But we'll show them that we're as good as the boys."

"I can take our football shirts and change the colour from grey," Layla said.

"Great!" Naomie replied. "But we still need money."

"We can sell cakes," I said.

Charligh looked like she was eating a lemon. "Do you remember your hot chilli cake?"

"Don't talk about that!" I answered.

"It's not a bad thing," said Layla. "Everything that we're doing now is because you made that terrible cake, and you couldn't dance."

That's one of the things that I love about Layla – she always looks for the bright side in everything.

"Let's have a pizza sale!" I said, suddenly.

Then, Layla had a better idea. "Let's make dessert pizzas. You know, pizzas with sweet things on top."

Everybody loved the idea. We decided to do it on Saturday at Layla's house. We needed a lot of different things for the pizzas. Everybody agreed to bring something. We needed to sell a lot of pizzas at two pounds a slice.

"We always have lots of bananas and other fruit at my house," said Talia. "I'll bring some."

We told Rhiannon about our plan. "I'll put some flyers in the library," she said. "And I'll put it on my Instagram, too."

I was beginning to feel brighter. Maybe I wasn't good at dancing or making cakes but I could still show everyone that I was a star.

"Zach and his friends will see that they were wrong," I thought. "Dad's eyes will stop being sad. And Mãe will be proud of me, and she'll remember me more often."

―――――――

That Saturday, we worked hard. We cooked our first pizzas at 11 a.m. Layla's mum helped us with the first one, and then we cooked the other pizzas very carefully.

At noon, we had a lot of different pizzas and they all smelled wonderful. We put plates over them because we didn't want them to get cold.

Twenty minutes later, Layla's front garden was full of customers.

"Well done, girls!" a man said. "This pizza smells better than the pizzas in the best restaurants in town." He bought two slices of pizza and gave us five pounds. "Keep the pound," he said. "You've worked hard."

The lunchtime customers left just after 3 p.m.! Steph, Talia and I made more pizzas in the next two hours. The afternoon customers arrived at around 5 p.m. There were more people than before.

"Oh no!" said Charligh. "It's Rosie and Erica."

I was surprised when they each bought a slice of the fruit pizza.

"I hope that you go to the tournament," Rosie said. She smiled the smile that she gives before saying something horrible. "You'll lose, and then we can all laugh. You were a terrible dancer. You and your team are losers – you can't win anything."

I stepped near her angrily, but Steph stopped me.

"Don't," she said. "They're not important enough to get angry with."

"That's right," said Allie. She hit her left hand with her right hand very hard. This frightened

Erica and she jumped. "We're going to **smash** it on the football field," Allie said, loudly. Rosie and Erica quickly ran away.

We sold our last pizza, cleaned the kitchen and then sat down at the table. Dad gave us five pounds for working hard, but we needed nearly ninety pounds more for the minibus.

Steph counted the money and wrote a number down. Then, Naomie counted the money again.

"I'm sorry," Naomie said. "But we didn't make ninety pounds." She smiled a secret smile at Steph. "We made one hundred and twelve pounds sixty!"

Everybody smiled and cheered.

"Bramrock Stars are going to the tournament," I thought.

———

Today was tournament day.

"We need to win all three of our games. There's no room for stupid mistakes," I thought.

We were in Group B and we had to play Windmill Villa, Brighton Dynamos and Hove Cosmos.

Windmill Villa and Brighton Dynamos were new teams like us, but everybody knew Hove Cosmos.

"They've played together for two years," I said. "They're really good."

"Oh no!" Charligh suddenly shouted. She was holding up our football shirts. They weren't grey now. They were worse – pink, brown and green mixed together! We all looked at Layla.

"What happened?" I asked.

"I tried to change the colour, but it went a bit wrong." Layla's face was red.

"A bit!" said Talia.

I put on one of the shirts. "It doesn't matter," I said. "We're here to WIN!"

We all put on our shirts. We looked horrible and we all laughed because it really didn't matter.

We walked on to the football field, and we were still laughing loudly.

———

We won our first game against Windmill Villa 3–0. I scored two of the goals! Brighton Dynamos were terrible, and we won 4–0.

"We need to win one more game and then we can go to the final in two weeks," I thought.

I was happy to see Mãe, Dad and Jordan standing together and cheering. We were a family again. Now it was time to win our last game.

CHAPTER SEVEN

Jaz Santos against the world

But our third game was very different. Hove Cosmos were faster and better than us in every way. At **half-time**, it was 2–0 to Cosmos. Then, to make things worse, it started to rain.

———

The second half started very badly. But then we discovered that Hove Cosmos couldn't play well on wet grass – and we could. Now I was happy that it was raining.

I scored our first goal after running between and round three of their players. Then, ten minutes later, Steph scored a goal. The final **score** was two – all. We didn't lose and we didn't win – it was a draw. But we needed three wins to be sure that we were in the final.

Before I could say anything, Miss Williams and Rhiannon arrived. Miss Williams was holding a yellow piece of paper. She was very excited. "This is your ticket to the final!" she said.

I couldn't speak. I carefully took the paper from her.

RESULT – BRAMROCK STARS FC
First game: Win – 3 points
Second game: Win – 3 points
Third game: Draw – 2 points
Total: 8 points
Congratulations! You are in the final.

"We did it!" said Allie. She was trying not to cry.

Mãe and Dad decided to have a special dinner because of our win, so we went home together.

The Bramrock Stars were in the final and my parents were being nice and not arguing.

Life was good.

———

That evening, Dad cooked dinner and we all ate together like a family. While Mum and Dad talked about boring things, Jordan and I washed the plates.

"Why are you so happy?" Jordan asked me.

"Look at Mãe and Dad." I smiled.

"You live in the clouds," he replied.

"What does Jordan know?" I thought. "He only thinks about music and band practice. I'm getting our parents to talk."

We finished washing the plates and went into the sitting room. Mãe and Dad were sitting on opposite sides of our big sofa and they were arguing again.

"Drew," Mãe said, "I'll do it. I've said it already. So please stop talking about it." She put her glass of orange juice down on the table – hard.

"Mãe, Dad . . ." I began. "Did you see me play?"

I didn't understand. Tonight was a **celebration**. Why weren't they happy?

"We're not children any more," Dad said to Mãe. "We're in our forties now. It's time to be an adult!"

They did not stop arguing. Mãe's voice got very loud, and Dad's became very quiet. I stood up.

"Two wins and a draw!" I shouted.

Mãe stopped in the middle of her sentence.

"Two wins and a draw," I repeated. "I scored the most goals and you two fight."

Mãe tried to hug me, but I stepped back. I didn't want her to touch me.

"I won those games to make everybody happy, but you and Dad never stop fighting."

"Jaz . . ." Mãe stopped. "I'm sorry," she said, finally. She looked at me, then at Dad and then at me again. "I'm making things worse," she said, but nobody answered. "I'm sorry. I'll go now," she said.

"Why are you sorry, Mãe?" I thought. "Are you sorry for leaving us, or sorry that you don't want to come back?"

I didn't know the answer. I didn't want to hear her "sorry". I wanted *her*.

After Mãe left, Dad tried to talk to me, but I ran upstairs to my bedroom. I hugged Kinsley, and then I cried and I cried, and I cried. Nobody understood me. I felt terrible.

———

It was me, Jaz Santos against the world.

And I was losing – *again!*

CHAPTER EIGHT
It's a lie!

The final was in two weeks so we decided to practise every lunchtime at school. We couldn't use the football field. "The boys have to practise for their games," Mr Roundtree said. So we practised at the end of the playground.

One day, after lunch, we had boring maths. Rosie and Erica came into the class late. They were looking at me and talking behind their hands at the same time. Then, Rosie went to talk to Mrs Forrest. Suddenly, Mrs Forrest called me to her desk. The class went quiet.

"Why did you do this?" Mrs Forrest pointed at something red on the left side of Rosie's face. "You hurt Rosie."

"It's not true. I didn't touch her," I said. "It's a lie."

"Rosie told me about it. You were practising outside, and you kicked your football into her face."

Steph, Naomie, Charligh and Talia tried to tell Mrs Forrest that it wasn't true.

"Erica saw everything," Mrs Forrest said.

I started to laugh. This wasn't a crime programme on TV.

"I'll give you something to laugh at," Mrs Forrest said. "You and your team can't play football at lunchtime!"

"I. Did. Not. Do. It," I said, slowly, but Mrs Forrest didn't listen.

Zach Bacon laughed at me, but Erica was much quieter than usual.

"Don't worry," said Charligh. "We'll practise more after school, OK?"

I thought about Rosie all day. Who hit her? I didn't know the answer. Rosie and Erica were always making problems, but I needed to **focus** on the tournament. Now we needed to practise even more after school because we couldn't play at lunchtimes.

On Wednesday, we went to the park. Talia wanted us to practise **penalties**.

"It's your turn now, Jaz," Rhiannon said.

But then I remembered Dad taking a penalty last year. He got hurt very badly and he had to stop playing football. Suddenly, I felt afraid to take the penalty. I tried to focus, but I couldn't, and I kicked the ball straight into Allie's hands. I was very unhappy because everybody scored a penalty, but not me. I tried not to worry, but inside I felt terrible.

"Are you OK, Jaz?" asked Rhiannon. "You're unhappy – your head isn't here today."

Rhiannon wasn't like some of my teachers. She wasn't angry with me – she wanted to understand my problems. I was sad because Rosie lied, and now I couldn't play football at lunchtime. I was angry because everybody thought that the boys' team was more important than the girls' team. I was worried because my parents couldn't stop arguing. But, most of all, I was unhappy because I wasn't good enough. Nothing I did was quite good enough.

"Have you ever been frightened about something that you can't change?" I asked Rhiannon. My voice was very small and quiet now. "How can I stop feeling like that?"

"Sometimes," Rhiannon said, "you have to be brave in your own way. You have to look at the thing that frightens you in the eye."

Rhiannon was kind, but she didn't really understand. Football stopped me from feeling angry and sad all the time because Mãe wasn't at home.

———

The next Monday at school we had art.

"We're going to do something special," Miss Williams said. "Work in pairs and paint a picture of your favourite heroes. The winners will show their picture to a famous artist. Mrs Forrest will look at the pictures and she'll choose the best."

I worked with Charligh, but our picture wasn't very good. "Rosie will win," I thought. "She's good at drawing and Mrs Forrest loves her."

Mrs Forrest looked at all the paintings, and then she said, "And the winners are . . . Rosie and Erica!"

"We did it!" Rosie shouted. "We won."

"Let's cheer for Rosie and Erica," Mrs Forrest said.

The **cheers** sounded like a storm in my head. "Everybody wants a daughter like Rosie," I thought. "Even Mãe doesn't want a daughter like me!"

Rosie was still smiling like she was better than everybody. I was so angry that I drew all over her picture with green paint. I waited for Rosie to shout at me or pull my hair. But she did something much worse – she cried.

Have you ever done something horrible and then felt bad? I felt very bad now.

It was very quiet in the class and Mrs Forrest quickly turned round.

"Jasmina Santos-Campbell, you get worse every day!" said Mrs Forrest.

I wanted to say "sorry" to Rosie. I wanted to say, "I did it because I was angry and because you lied about your face." But I didn't say anything.

"Your football final is in four days." Mrs Forrest stood very close to me. "I hope that your friends enjoy it, because *you* won't play!"

I couldn't believe that this was happening. This was the end of my football **dream**.

———

It was break time and I was sitting with my friends. Everybody was sad and nobody looked at me.

"What happened?" asked Allie.

"Jaz did something horrible to Rosie's painting," said Talia.

"Now I can't go to the final on Friday," I said.

"I've been good for weeks," Allie said. "Why weren't you good, too?"

"This is *our* dream, too," Charligh said, "but you've killed it. I stopped going to dance class to help you and the Stars! But you only think about Jasmina Santos-Campbell!"

It really hurt to hear my best friend say my full name like that.

"I'm going to make things better," I said.

———————

That evening, I watched a crime programme with Dad. In one story, a man wanted people to like him. He asked his friends to break the windows in his house. After this happened a lot of times, people were sorry for him and they liked him more. This made me think about Rosie. I thought about Rosie's face, and I knew the answer.

CHAPTER NINE
Surprise!

The next morning, I stopped Erica in the road near my house. She was going to school.

"Why did Rosie do it?" I asked. "And why did you help her?"

Erica looked like she was going to cry. "If Rosie asks me to do something I have to do it, or she won't be my friend," she said. "Rosie wants people to feel sorry for her. She's worried that she won't remember the dance for *Spinning Alices*. Her mum's tired and angry all the time because she has a new baby. She doesn't have time for Rosie. If Rosie doesn't tell lies about other people, nobody will think about her. We tried to play football like your team, but I kicked the ball and it hit her in her face. It was a mistake."

Erica looked at me. She had kind eyes.

"What are you going to do?" she asked.

I didn't know. I felt sorry for Rosie. Her parents didn't have time for her. I understood that. Rosie and I were different but, in some ways, we were the same.

We got to school, and I stopped at the door. Everybody was already in their classrooms.

"You go inside first, Erica," I said. "I don't want Rosie to be angry with you."

———

At break time, I told Miss Williams my problems.

"Parents don't always agree. I'm certain that your mother doesn't hate your father. And your father doesn't hate your mother," she said after listening carefully. "They haven't forgotten you."

"It's not fair that Rosie always wins," I said. "But I want to do something to her painting. I want it to be as good as new again."

Miss Williams helped me to mix the paint colours and then I worked on Rosie's painting all through break.

———

Rosie, Erica and I stayed behind after school. I showed Rosie the painting.

"I'm really sorry about your painting, Rosie," I said. "I've tried to make it better."

"I love it!" Rosie said and then she kissed the air on both sides of my face. "Mwah! Mwah!"

"When can you play football again?" asked Mãe.

"I don't know," I said. We were talking on the phone, and I wanted to tell her everything. "How can I tell her that there is something wrong inside me?" I thought. "And there are always problems around me because of that."

"You made one mistake," Mãe said. "This doesn't mean that you have to forget your dream."

"You're right," I said. "If I play football, everything feels better."

"I'm sorry that I argued with Dad after the match," Mãe said.

"It's OK," I said.

"This weekend, let's **celebrate** our dreams," Mãe said. "Even if we make a mistake!"

On Wednesday, Mrs Forrest called me to her office. I was a bit frightened and I felt sick. "What have I done wrong now?" I thought.

I knocked on the door. I was very surprised to hear Miss Williams's voice. "Come in," she said.

"I'm sorry," I said, after I stepped inside.

"Don't worry, Jaz," Miss Williams said. "You haven't done anything wrong. *We* want to say sorry to *you*."

"Why?" I asked.

Miss Williams looked at Mrs Forrest. After a minute, Mrs Forrest started to speak.

"Jasmina . . . We . . . didn't know that Erica kicked the ball at Rosie. We were . . . um . . . wrong . . ."

"This morning, Rosie and Erica came to the office," Miss Williams said. "Erica spoke to Rosie and then Rosie came here and told the truth. You made Rosie's painting better. Now Rosie wants you to play in the final, but *we* also want you to play in the final on Friday." She looked at Mrs Forrest. "This is a good lesson about looking at things in a different way."

How could a week that started badly end this well?

———

"In. Out. In. Out. Are you sure that you're in the team again and that we can win this tournament on Friday?" asked Talia. Everybody laughed and cheered. Mrs Forrest came to our table and told us to be quiet.

I said sorry to my friends.

"It's been difficult for me," I said. "My parents argued a lot and now my mother is living with her sister. Things are terrible at home."

Steph gave me a big warm **hug**.

"It's not easy," said Allie. "I live with my mum, and I don't see my dad very often. I feel terrible, too, sometimes."

I felt better after talking to my friends. Now, some of them understood me.

———

That evening, after our training, Dad said, "I've got a surprise for everybody."

He pulled the most beautiful football shirts I've ever seen from his bag. They were dark purple and they had three purple stars above the words, BRAMROCK STARS FC. Then, he gave us some purple football socks and some purple shorts.

"I LOVE THEM!" Charligh shouted.

"Jaz's mum made these," Dad said.

I nearly cried. We all had numbers on the backs of our shirts. Mine was number three. We were a real team, and these shirts were ours!

———

At home, I had a video call with Mãe. I put my shorts and shirt on.

"You can do it," Mãe said. "Shoot for the stars!" Then, we said goodbye.

There was one last thing to do.

———

After dinner, I went into the garden with Dad to practise penalties. I kicked the ball – right into his hands.

"Try again, Jaz," he said.

For ten minutes, I tried again and again. Each time, Dad saved my penalty. I wanted to walk away, but I remembered Rhiannon. She wanted me to be brave.

I tried again and again, until finally – I scored.

"Good shot!" said Dad.

I missed a lot of shots before I scored that goal. The important thing was that I wasn't so afraid any more.

CHAPTER TEN
Shoot for the stars

It was the final: Bramrock Stars FC vs the Silverton Shiners. The Shiners' star player was a girl called Jilly. She tried to score in the first minute of the game, but the ball went over the goal. Soon after that, I had the ball. Talia stood near the goal and three Shiners quickly ran at her. Nobody was looking at me and I quickly kicked the ball into the left corner of the goal. It was 1−0 to us!

I was excited, happy and frightened – all at the same time. I touched the stars on my shirt. I was the team captain. I needed to help them play our very best game.

_____

The whistle blew and the game started again. The Shiners started playing dirty because they were losing. Suddenly, something hit my leg. It was the boot of one of the Shiners players.

"What are you doing?" I asked her.

"Kicking you," said the girl. Then, she "stole" the ball and kicked it to someone in her team.

"Did you see that?" I looked at the referee, but she didn't do anything.

The Shiners kept trying to pass the ball to Jilly, but Steph stopped them each time. Then, Jilly kicked Steph's ankle as hard as she could. Steph fell down and started to cry.

"I'm OK," she said, but we all knew that she was not.

"Don't worry," said the first-aid man. He moved Steph's left ankle from side to side.

"That's the wrong ankle!" cried Steph.

"You'll be OK, Steph," Dad said. "We've called your mum."

It was horrible to see her. Steph always looked after everyone, and now her ankle hurt badly.

––––––

"Where's your substitute?" the referee asked. Most teams have a substitute player – she comes on the field if a player has to leave the game.

"We don't have a substitute," I said.

"Next time, bring a substitute," the referee replied. "Now your team only has six players! And you." She turned to Jilly. "Yellow card! Do that again and I'll give you a red card. Then your team will only have six players, too!"

The referee gave the Bramrock Stars a free kick because Jilly got a yellow card. This meant that we could kick the ball anywhere on the field.

Talia took the free kick. Layla was waiting in midfield and Talia kicked the ball to her, but the Shiners quickly took the ball from Layla. They were hungry to win, and they played harder and dirtier than before. Allie was great. She saved five goals, one after another. But then, just before half-time, the Shiners scored a goal.

During the half-time break, Miss Williams and Rhiannon brought us oranges and water.

"They're stronger than you are," Miss Williams said, "and they've also played more football. You must fight as a team, then you can win. Your strengths are different from the Shiners'."

"They think that they'll score another goal and win very easily," I said, "because we only have six players. But they don't play like a team, and we do. That's our strength. Listen! I have an idea."

———

The Shiners quickly scored another goal in the second half. Now it was 2–1 to them. They hugged and celebrated on the field for a long time.

After that, they played safe – they didn't try to score, they only defended.

"Two minutes!" Rhiannon shouted.

It was time for our plan.

I ran down the right wing and passed the ball to Talia. For a second, she looked from me to the goal. "Follow the plan, Talia," I thought. I moved to a good position to score, and the Shiners' defenders and their goalkeeper all ran at me. Nobody was looking at Talia. She kicked the ball past the defenders and at the goal. The goalkeeper tried to change her direction. Now it was a race between the ball and the goalkeeper . . .

GOAL!

Our plan worked and the game finished 2–2. Now it was time for penalties.

"The first team to score three goals wins the game," the referee said.

Both teams scored two penalties each.

Victoria Chatton was the last Shiners player to take a penalty. She kicked the ball – too low and too wide. Allie easily saved it. The score was still two all. Now it was my turn for a penalty.

My mouth was dry, and my hands were wet. "Focus!" I thought. There were many voices in my head: "You never learn!" "You can do this . . ." "You can't . . ."

Focus! Shoot . . . for . . . the . . . Stars!

I kicked the ball, and it went over the line and into the back of the net. Suddenly, the referee was blowing her whistle and people were cheering loudly because . . .

We . . . did . . . it!

Dad gave me a big hug and then the Bramrock Stars spoke to Gayle Gallagher, a writer from the *Brighton Chronicle* newspaper.

"How do you feel?" she asked us.

"It feels wonderful," Charligh said. Then, all the Bramrock Stars spoke to Gayle.

"Is there anything more that you want to say?" Gayle asked at the end.

"You can call us the Dream Team!" I said.

———

An hour later, Alana Young gave us our medals and trophy. In the past, Alana was a professional football player. She invited the Bramrock Stars to a special training practice after Christmas. Then, Rhiannon said, "Steph's mum says her ankle isn't too bad. She'll be able to play football again after Christmas."

———

Finally, it was time to go home.

"I sent Mãe a video of the penalties," Dad said, smiling.

"My dream has come true today," I said.

───────

At home, there was a banner on the wall above the stairs. It said, "Congratulations, Jaz!" Then, I saw Mãe. She was holding a very strange cake. It was high on one side and low on the other.

On the cake, it said,

Congratulations!
To our Jaz –
Always Shoot for the Stars!

We all looked at the cake and then laughed. Mum gave me the first slice. It was made with love, and it was wonderful!

———

It was Christmas. Mãe and I were having dinner together. Mãe sat next to me.

"Are you sad that you have a daughter like me?" I asked. "Because I do everything wrong?"

Mãe looked at me with surprise. "I'm so happy to have the kindest, bravest, funniest daughter in the world." She smiled at me. "I think that you'll play for England one day. What makes me happy? You, Jaz. Win or lose, you're always a star." Then, she kissed the top of my head.

———

"Mãe might not come home," I thought. "But she's always here for me."

I looked up at the sky. Sometimes, it was difficult to shoot for the stars, but it was always important to try.

During-reading questions

CHAPTER ONE

1 Which year is Jaz in at her dance class?
2 What happens when Rosie eats Jaz's cake?

CHAPTER TWO

1 Where does Jaz often have dinner on Fridays?
2 How did the fire start?
3 Why does Jordan open Jaz's bedroom window, do you think?

CHAPTER THREE

1 How many girls does Jaz invite to her sleepover?
2 What is Layla's favourite colour?

CHAPTER FOUR

1 Why does Tia hold the front door wide open?
2 Who does Jaz ask to coach her team?
3 How many followers does Rhiannon have on Instagram?

CHAPTER FIVE

1 What does "stealing" the ball mean, do you think?
2 How many times did Rachel Yankey play for England?
3 Who throws rubbish all over the girls?

CHAPTER SIX

1 Why do the girls want to make pizzas?
2 How much money do the girls make from pizzas?
3 How long have Hove Cosmos played together?

CHAPTER SEVEN

1 When does it start to rain?
2 What does "to live in the clouds" mean, do you think?
3 How does Mãe feel about two wins and a draw?

CHAPTER EIGHT

1 Where is Rosie hurt?
2 Why is it difficult for Jaz to take a penalty?
3 When is the football final?

CHAPTER NINE

1 Who does Jaz talk to at break time?
2 What is Dad's surprise after training?
3 How many stars are there on each football shirt?

CHAPTER TEN

1 Who kicks Steph's ankle?
2 How many goals does Allie save in the first half?

After-reading questions

1 Is *Jaz Santos vs the World* a happy story or a sad story? Why?
2 Which character was your least favourite in this story?
  Why?
3 Look back at your answers to "Before-reading question 2".
  Were you right?
4 Choose one of these characters. Why does Jaz like or not
  like them? How is she different from them?
  a Rosie Calderwood   **b** Erica   **c** Zach Bacon

Exercises

1 **Who says these words? Who do they say them to?**
Write the correct names in your notebook.

1 "This is our last chance to show Ms Morgan that we can dance well." *Jaz to Charligh*

2 "You can come back in five minutes."

3 "Do you want me to cook something?"

4 "Ms Morgan thinks that I can be one of the best dancers."

5 "It's very late."

6 "Rosie makes the best cakes."

7 "Try it."

8 "Jaz did it."

2 **Write questions for these answers in your notebook.**

1 Who *shouted at Jaz?*	Mrs Forrest shouted at Jaz.
2 Where	Jaz often went to dinner at Charligh's house on Fridays.
3 Who	Jordan was at band practice.
4 What	Mãe was smoking a cigarette in the garden.
5 Who	Dad had a red face.
6 Where	Jordan sat on the floor in Jaz's bedroom.
7 Who	Jaz fell on the wet grass.
8 What	Dad made two cups of hot chocolate.

3 **Complete these sentences in your notebook, using the adverbs from the box.**

suddenly	carefully	well
quickly	easily	nearly

1 Jaz ___suddenly___ had an idea.
2 It was .... dark when Jordan and Jaz left their house.
3 Jaz did not know Talia very ....
4 Talia .... read Jaz's card.
5 Allie was always in trouble at school because she got angry very ....
6 Layla .... forgot that she was in Jaz's team.

4 **Complete these sentences in your notebook, using the words from the box.**

coach	skill	positions
practice	training	captain

Jaz and her friends started a football team called the Bramrock Stars. They needed a ¹ ___coach___ to help them play better football. Jaz was very happy to be the ² .... of the Bramrock Stars. She wanted her team to play a 2-2-2 formation, but her friends did not like their ³ .... They did not play well at their first ⁴ .... and everybody was angry. After that, Rhiannon helped the Bramrock Stars to play better football. The Bramrock Stars learned about their strengths and talked about what they wanted to do most in their ⁵ .... Jaz's. ⁶ .... was dribbling.

5 **Write the correct word in your notebook and then match it with its definition.**

Example: 1 – d

1 ebidrlb ....*dribble*....   **a** when you are trying very hard to do something and you only think about this thing

2 airnt ....   **b** Other people try to do and say the same things as this person because they are a good example to follow.

3 ofcus ....   **c** to do a thing well

4 lore ledom ....   **d** to move a ball while you run by kicking it again and again

5 runt ....   **e** not frightened

6 sllfkui ....   **f** when you practise for a sport

7 reabv ....   **g** Some people do a thing. Now you must or can do this thing, too.

6 Complete these sentences in your notebook, using the comparative or superlative form of the adjectives in the box.

| good | bad | ugly | expensive | horrible |
| good | cheap | bright |

1 The girls' football team is ....*better*.... than the boys' football team.
2 The .... thing was the minibus.
3 The .... minibus cost forty pounds an hour.
4 Our football shirts are the .... in the competition.
5 Layla's idea for sweet pizzas was .... than Jaz's idea.
6 Jaz felt .... because making pizzas was a good plan.
7 The pink, brown and green football shirts were .... than before.
8 Windmill Villa played .... than the Bramrock Stars, so they lost the game.

7 Are these sentences *true* or *false*? Write the correct answers in your notebook.

1 Hove Cosmos were faster than the Bramrock Stars. ....*true*....
2 It was 2–0 to the Bramrock Stars at half-time.
3 Steph scored the first goal.
4 Rhiannon gave Jaz a yellow piece of paper.
5 Jordan and Jaz washed the plates.
6 Jaz shouted, "Two draws and a win!"
7 After Dad left, Jaz hugged Kinsley.

8 **Write the correct verb form, *past simple* or *past continuous*, in your notebook.**

The Bramrock Stars ¹ ....*needed*.... (**need**) to practise football every day before the final game, but Mr Roundtree ² .... (**not let**) them use the football field. One day, Jaz ³ .... (**talk**) to Charligh, when Rosie ⁴ .... (**tell**) Mrs Forrest a lie. Mrs Forrest ⁵ .... (**not believe**) Jaz. She only believed Rosie. This ⁶ .... (**make**) Jaz sad. Later, Jaz ⁷ .... (**tell**) Rhiannon her problems while the other girls ⁸ .... (**play**) football. When Rosie ⁹ .... (**win**) a painting competition, Jaz ¹⁰ .... (**feel**) very angry because Rosie smiled like she was better than everybody. Jaz ¹¹ .... (**not like**) this, so she ¹² .... (**draw**) all over Rosie's painting.

9 **What happened here? Match in your notebook.**

Example: 1 − e

1 Jaz talks to Erica.

2 Miss Williams listens to Jaz's problems.

3 Rosie kisses Jaz.

4 Miss Williams and Mrs Forrest say sorry to Jaz.

5 Dad gives everyone a new football shirt.

6 Jaz practises penalties.

a After football training

b In the garden

c In Mrs Forrest's office

d In the art room after school

e In the road

f At school in break time

10 **Complete these sentences in your notebook, using the names from the box.**

Jilly	Jaz	Rhiannon	Talia	The Referee
		Mãe	Miss Williams	

1 ...*Jilly*... kicked Steph's ankle as hard as she could.

2 .... gave the Bramrock stars a free kick.

3 .... and .... brought the team oranges and water.

4 "You can call us the Dream Team!" said ....

5 .... kicked the ball past the defenders and into the goal.

6 .... said that she thinks Jaz will play for England one day.

Project work

1 Make a poster for a football competition for students your age.

2 Write a newspaper report for the final football game that the Bramrock Stars play.

3 It is the day of the cake cooking class. Write a diary page for one of the following people:
   a Mrs Tavella
   b Rosie
   c Charligh.

An answer key for all questions and exercises can be found at **www.penguinreaders.co.uk**

Glossary

argue (v.); **argument** (n.)
when people talk to each other in an
angry way because they don't agree.
Argument is the noun of *argue*.

believe (v.); **believe in** (phr. v.)
You say "I couldn't *believe* it" if
you were very surprised about
something and thought that it
shouldn't happen. If you *believe in*
something, you think that it is a
good and right thing.

brave (adj.)
A *brave* person is not frightened.

captain (n.)
the most important person in a
sports *team*

celebrate (v.); **celebration** (n.)
when you do something nice
because a good thing has happened
and you are very happy about it.
Celebration is the noun of *celebrate*.

cheer (v. and n.)
to shout because you are happy
about something. *Cheer* is the noun
of *cheer*.

cinnamon (n.)
Cinnamon is brown and comes from a
tree. You use it in cooking.

coach (v. and n.)
to *coach* someone is to teach them a
sport or other *skill*. A *coach's* job is to
coach people.

congratulations (phr.)
You say "*Congratulations!*" to
someone to show that you are happy
that they have done something
good, or that something good has
happened to them.

customer (n.)
Customers buy things.

dream (n.)
A *dream* is like a hope. You want it to
happen but it may not be possible.

dribble (v.)
to move a ball while you run by
kicking it again and again

elephant (n.)
a very big grey animal from Africa
or India with large ears and a very
long nose

fair (adj.)
Something is right or it is the same
for everyone. It is *fair*.

final (n. and adj.); **finally** (adv.)
The *final* is the last part of a sports
tournament, when a person or *team*
wins. The *final* thing is the last one
before the end. *Finally* means after
a long time. You can also say *finally*
before saying the last thing after two
or more things.

flyer (n.)
a small piece of paper. It gives
information about something.

focus (n. and v.)
when you are trying very hard to do something and you only think about this thing. *Focus* is the verb of *focus*.

half-time (n.)
the time between the two halves of a sports game, when the players rest

hug (v. and n.)
If you *hug* someone or give someone a *hug*, you put your arms round them because you love them or like them a lot.

keepy-uppy (n.)
when you stop a football from hitting the ground by kicking it up again and again

lie (v. and n.)
You say something but it is not true. You are *lying* or telling a *lie*.

make-up (n.)
special colours for your face. You use *make-up* to look different or more beautiful.

miss (v.)
1) You are sad because a person is not with you. You *miss* the person.
2) You try to catch a ball or hit something in a sport but you can't do it. You *miss* the *shot*.

newspaper (n.)
You read about the news in a *newspaper*.

pass (v.)
If you *pass* the ball in a sport, you kick, throw or hit it to another player in your *team*.

penalty (n.)
when a player can try to *score* a goal without other players trying to take the ball from them

position (n.)
Every player in a sports *team* has a place on a sports field. This is the player's *position*.

practise (v.); **practice** (n.)
You do something a lot and then you can do it well. You *practise*. *Practice* is the noun of *practise*.

prize (n.)
If you win a *prize* for doing something, you get money or a nice thing.

professional (adj.)
A *professional* player is very good at their sport and gets money for playing it.

proud (adj.)
If you are *proud* of a person, they have done something good and you feel very happy about it.

role model (n.)
If a person is a *role model*, other people try to do and say the same things as them because they are a good example to follow.

score (v. and n.)
to *score* is to get a point (= a number for showing that a person or *team* is doing well or winning) in a game. The *final score* is the number of points for each person or *team* at the end of the game.

shoot (v.); **shot** (n.)
to *shoot* is to try to *score* in a sport by kicking, throwing or hitting the ball. A *shot* is when you *shoot* in a sport.

show (n.)
when people act, dance, sing or play music and other people watch them. You watch a *show* in a theatre or on television.

skill (n.); **skilful** (adj.)
A *skilled* person has learned to do a thing well. This thing is a *skill*. The person is *skilful*.

smash (v.)
If you *smash it*, you do something very well, like winning a game or being the best.

star (n.)
1) If you reach for the *stars*, you try to be good at a difficult thing.
2) A *star* dancer, player, etc., is better than all the other people in that group, *team*, etc.
3) a very famous actor, player, etc.

strength (n.)
You are very good at something. This thing is your *strength*.

team (n.)
a group of people playing sport or working together

tournament (n.)
In a *tournament*, people play a lot of games. The winners play against other winners. In the end, there is only one *team* left. This *team* is the winner of the *tournament*.

train (v.); **training** (n.)
when you *practise* for a sport. *Training* is the noun of *train*.

turn (n.)
Some people do a thing. Now you must or can do this thing, too. It is your *turn*.

video (n.)
moving pictures on television, a computer, camera, etc.

whole (adj.)
all of something